THE RESCUE OF JULES VERNE

THE RESCUE OF JULES VERNE

A HOLLOW EARTH SHORT STORY

ROBERT J. MCCARTER

LITTLE HUMMINGBIRD PUBLISHING

FOREWORD

This story is available with a number of other stories of mine in one of my collections (just in case you'd like a bunch of stories to read):

- Creatures Featured: Thirteen Stories of Monsters and other Creatures

THE RESCUE OF JULES VERNE

A HOLLOW EARTH STORY

A world within our world. A secret tunnel hidden under the Eiffel Tower. A small central sun at the center of our planet warming those lands in the hollow earth. Seas with no horizon because of the concave nature of those lands. Adventures beyond the imagination of the modern man at the dawning of the twentieth century.

All these things would have sounded preposterous when the little man approached. I was in Paris for the 1889 World's Fair looking at the mighty tower that Gustave Eiffel had just erected, his graceful iron girders rising up into the air. This appeared to be the pinnacle of engineering, a bar which mankind would have to strive mightily to top. Eiffel had a hand in the glorious Statue of Liberty that overlooked my home and now this. I was hoping to find a chance to meet him.

The people swirled about me, glorious smells from the food stalls tantalized me, and there was laughter in the spring air as I stood on the Champ de Mars staring at Eiffel's tower. Four iron feet set broadly apart forming a sensible square, graceful arches between those mighty legs. The four edges of the tower slowly thinning and sweeping up to a glorious point over a thousand feet above me.

"Beautiful, no?" he asked, his breath smelling of garlic, his body of sweat. I barely glanced at the short man, noticing that his waistcoat was not buttoned and he had no hat to cover his unruly shock of red hair. He was badly in need of a barber and overdue for a bath.

I grunted and kept staring at Gustave's mighty achievement.

"You are Marco Walker, no?"

That got my attention and I met the little man's hungry eyes.

"Monsieur Eiffel asks for the pleasure of your company, if you will but follow me."

He then walked away without a backward glance. Never one to look a gift horse in the mouth or to shy away from an adventure, I followed him.

~

*G*ustave Eiffel was well dressed with his greying hair unruly, his beard trimmed, but not well trimmed, and his clothing expensive but a tad dirty. He looked to be a man that had too much to do. His eyes, though, are what drew me in. He had the look of a man who was constantly tired, but such intelligence. We sat in a great hall beneath the tower, the curved roof and iron girders echoing the design of the base of the tower above us. I had passed through a hallway full of large portraits, some I recognized. Jules Verne, the writer, Theodore Roosevelt, the governor of New York, Gertrude Bell, a well-known archeologist.

"Where did the dinosaurs go to?" Eiffel asked across the great wooden table from me as he poured wine for both of us. "Or, for that matter, where did they come from? How many religions speak of a realm underneath us? Hell, Purgatory, Naraka. What of lost lands like Agartha, Shamballa, or Atlantis?

"What if each of them had a bit of truth in them, and each of those bits speaks of the same truth? What if there was a world within our world from which all those legends sprang? What if I told you there was a society that has been secretly exploring these realms for millennia?"

He waited, his breath coming fast, smelling of tobacco, and his cheeks flushed from the effort.

"I'd say you were mad," I replied with a broad smile, taking a sip of his marvelous wine.

Eiffel told me many preposterous things that afternoon. Things I scoffed at. Things that I didn't believe. Things that all turned out to be true.

The pictures in the hallway were all members of this Hollow Earth Society. They saw themselves as the guardians and protectors of the land inside the earth. Eiffel's tower had been built as a cover for the tunnel they had dug all the way through. Before the tunnel, the only way down were natural caverns that were dangerous and took months to traverse, and survival was a hard thing to secure.

"The Earth's crust is 650 to 800 kilometers thick, and sandwiched at its center is an eight-kilometer-thick band of dense metal," Eiffel said. "It is an element harder than a diamond and denser than anything we've ever seen, the stuff of stars it must be. There are several natural holes in this layer, one of them right beneath us."

I shrugged, not convinced. "You still haven't explained gravity. How the earth can be hollow. How this central sun can be in the middle of our planet and we don't just fall into it."

He sighed as if tiring of teaching a dunce of a pupil. "It's this band of metal," he said, waving his wineglass at me with such enthusiasm that he slopped some of the red liquid on the table. "It makes the earth strong enough to be hollow. It is so dense it generates the bulk of the gravity that affects us here on the surface, as well as in the hollow interior, which is why we call it gravitinium. But we must not debate this, my friend. Before long you will experience how there is no gravity within this band, or more specifically, gravity is canceled out when you are in it, and how your feet will hold to the inner surface of our planet."

They were desperate. The tunneling had been much more expensive and much more difficult than they thought. They needed funds very soon or they would lose control over the tower, and the tunnel, and thus the hollow earth. To address this crisis, Jules Verne had ventured into the hollow earth alone, and after three weeks had not returned.

"Let me prove this to you," Eiffel said. "I will show you the tunnel and the machine that dug it."

~

*E*iffel's tunneling machine stank of coal smoke, belched steam, and was entirely too small. The outside was some four feet in diameter and the inside was barely half of that. He told me the hole had to be as narrow as possible, "It is 700 kilometers long, after all." The machine was twelve feet long, either end had a cylindrical rotating nose with teeth he claimed were diamond tipped, and the sides were lined with metal gears on short arms so that it could slow its fall during descent or use them to climb up.

It is the twin of the machine that drilled the great long tunnel. He called it "La Taupe," or "The Mole." He said there was always digging to be done, what with how either direction from that dense metal core strata was up and dirt would accumulate. The cursed machine was like a coffin inside and only carried one person.

"Down to the core will be easy and fast," he said after explaining the controls to me; a series of levers, a hole to peer in to see out the front of the craft, and tubes to breathe through to minimize the coal smoke. "Perhaps eight hours, no more, and very exciting. Up, I am afraid up is quite tedious; my little mole is a good climber, but not fast."

I held myself steady, but just looking at that machine made me sweat, the idea of locking myself into it was terrifying. This crazy Frenchman wanted me to strap myself into a coal-fired, steam-driven coffin and ride it all the way to what he claimed was a hollow Earth below our feet and then face unknown challenges in a violent and primitive land trying to rescue a man and secure a treasure he didn't know was there so that the Hollow Earth Society could survive. And I was violently claustrophobic, although I hadn't told him that.

"So, in the morning?" he asked with a grin.

I swallowed and nodded.

~

"I know what a man like you fears," Eiffel said with a small smile over our sumptuous dinner of roasted, stuffed duck, stuffing, creamed vegetables, and chocolate soufflé for dessert. And more wine, of course. "It is what a man like me fears."

I gestured for him to continue, chewing slowly on the delicious duck.

"We don't fear death or failure. We don't fear pain or loneliness." His tone became hushed as he leaned towards me. "We fear that our greatest achievements are behind us, that the creeping infirmities and indifferences of age will reach us and make us small." His breath smelled of the strong wine we had been drinking.

I bit my lip and nodded. He was right, for how was I to equal my time with James Chapman in South Africa or exploring China with Francis Younghusband, much less my youth fighting in America's Civil War. I had passed forty years of age, a most feared marker for men of spirit and adventure.

"I see it in your face, Monsieur Walker," he continued. "What I offer is nothing less than the greatest adventure known to mankind."

~

*W*hen morning came, I was far from ready to crawl into that contraption for two days. My palms were sweating and my heart racing just at the thought of it.

Eiffel patted the metal shell of his mole and said, "Your challenge is beyond difficult. Jules Verne—I am sure you must have heard of him—was on a mission of the utmost import. I would have preferred that we mounted an expedition, moved people and equipment down slowly, taken our time, but I am afraid our position is most desperate financially. Jules insisted that he go alone and the second mole be held in reserve in case of desperate need, which brings us to you, Monsieur Walker. In six months, we will have two more moles built, we will have established a base camp, but that will be too late for our great Hollow Earth Society.

"Your being here in Paris, now, is like a sign from God. If anyone can find him in this wild land below our feet, you can."

I smiled, still not quite sure this wasn't some kind of elaborate hoax, and studied Eiffel's face. He was a man carrying a burden, that was clear, and fatigue was written in his sallow, sagging skin, but I knew there was more he wasn't telling me, more that I would need to know if there was truly a hollow earth and I was to survive it.

"And what was Mr. Verne's mission?" I asked.

Eiffel's faced darkened and he gestured up. "This great tower above us was built here as a cover for our tunneling efforts. We had to do it quickly and drained all of our resources." He got up and walked to the sloped tunnel that the mole stood in front of. That tunnel quickly curved straight down, the cool air pouring out of it ruffling his hair. "It is essential that we retain possession of this tunnel and this knowledge. The knowledge of a hollow earth in the hands of less temperate men than us could be disastrous."

The mole room also had portraits of the members of the Hollow Earth Society. He walked to the photograph of Jules Verne where he was posing in front a model of the Nautilus submarine. "Some of his stories contain more truth than one would suspect," which brought to mind *The Journey to the Center of the Earth*. Eiffel sighed again and pulled a cigar from his pocket, bit one end off, spat it on the floor, and lit it, grey smoke curling up towards the ceiling.

"There is a well-known set of tunnels under the Great Pyramid of Giza. It is believed that the pharaoh Khufu built the pyramid, in part, to hide and control the passageway to the hollow earth. Jules went seeking some of Khufu's treasures which are believed to be hidden there."

~

"*Over seven hundred kilometers straight down, that's how far it is to the inside,*" *Eiffel said that night during dinner where he lectured me about many things that seemed absurd until I found myself experiencing them.* "*The caverns of the past made that distance thousands of kilometers and took months to traverse relying on whatever sources of water could be found and whatever food could be taken. Now you will go straight down*"—*he paused and chuckled*—"*and then straight up again. We mustn't forget the gravitinium, and it will only take two days.*"

I would like to report that after expeditions in Africa, China, and surviving a terrible war that tore a country apart, not to mention growing up in the wilds of Alaska, that the hollow earth was easily mastered, but that would not be the truth.

When Eiffel's cursed mole finally released me from its

cloying grip, I was nearly mad. Two days of stale, stinking air. Two days of its rumbling progress, first too fast as we flew down and then too slow as we crawled up. Two days of nothing but water to drink and a bottle to piss in.

The fresh air was a relief and I sucked it in through the open hatchway. Looking up I noticed just how very strange the sky was, with its thousands-mile thick atmosphere. I did not see clouds, per se, but above me was a thick, grey, unchanging expanse, with an orange-yellow ball burning at its center.

I crawled out of my prison, my hands shaking, and jumped to the verdant ground. My legs failed me and I went down in an awkward heap. I took a deep breath and smelled something floral and noticed just how damp the air was. I distracted myself by staring about me at the landscape that at first seemed familiar, but then became more and more foreign.

There is no horizon when you are on the inside of a sphere. In all directions, if you can but see far enough, is more land or ocean—yes, there are vast oceans there. Eiffel's tunnel ended in a deep, verdant valley filled with tall grasses, low bushes, and over-sized ferns. My mole sat next to another, the one Verne had taken down here. As much as I hated these things, I went over and examined his, finding nothing out of place, but I did find a set of boot tracks in the moist soil that circled around the craft, went to the large hole in the ground that I had just come out of, and then set strongly off towards the...

And here is another problem with this confounded hollow earth. I could not tell the direction. North would be towards the north pole, but from the inside with the central sun ever unmoving right above you, how do you tell?

I pulled my compass out and was relieved to find that there was indeed a north in this strange land, the tracks I had found led towards the southeast. I took a moment to eat some rations —even French army rations are a cut above the rest of the world's—and let my stomach settle and recover from my long rumbling journey. I strapped on my machete and Colt 45 and hoisted the backpack on my shoulders. I also took the odd metal walking stick that Eiffel insisted that I have with me at all times.

With a deep breath, I headed out to explore the hollow earth.

❧

*I*f I were a naturalist, I could spend pages and pages explaining how the flora and fauna in the hollow earth differed from its outer earth counterparts. How similar and at the same time how very different. I might theorize that the fewer species of both flora and fauna are the result of how isolated this place is and the difficulty of traveling from the outer earth to the inner.

I might go on and on until you were bored and desperate to know about Jules Verne and the lost Egyptian treasure. But I am no naturalist. What I can tell you is that the land was verdant and jungle-like, that the landscape could change dramatically and quickly, that the insects—all I saw that first day—were considerably larger than on the outside.

Verne's trail was not hard to follow, it led resolutely to the southeast over rolling valleys of tall grass lined by thick forest with trees three hundred feet tall. In the shade of the trees grew ferns taller than a man.

As I walked through the unforested valleys, I came across frequent areas of blackened earth that puzzled me greatly until I survived my first hollow earth thunderstorm.

Rain came and went quickly, the humidity always high, the temperature in the mid-seventies, the sun a glow through the grey always directly above. The never moving central sun shaped much of what was different about this land. If a plant was in the sun, it was always in the sun, if it was in the shade, it was always in the shade.

The first day was a marvel. The tunnel opening was in a deep valley, and when I emerged out of it I was greeted with a sight that is too spectacular to describe. Mountains, higher than the Himalayas, thrusting towards that central sun, tall and verdant to the top, and not one bit of snow. Rivers running down those mountains into wide oceans. The land itself green as far as the eye could see. And the eye could see far. There was no horizon, the land gently curving up until it was swallowed by the grey of the moist sky.

To the south, almost hidden by the moist air, was a volcano, tall and wide, spitting out globs of lava that fell hissing into the ocean that had formed around it. I felt a faint rumbling under my feet and had no doubt this monster of a volcano was its cause. The land there was not green but the dark of newly formed volcanic land with three stripes of red flowing down its sides into the ocean.

When I saw that view so spectacular, I leaned on the metal cane, a dizziness having descended on me. I think that until that moment, I hadn't believed that I was on the inside of our great planet. Until I saw the land curving up in the distance instead of disappearing into the horizon, I couldn't believe that the earth was hollow and a great and wild land was below all our feet as we go about our days on the outside.

A wall of wind hit me hard and I caught a whiff of ozone. I looked a bit towards the south and saw a storm rolling my way. The clouds were differentiated from the normal smoky grey of the sky as a roiling darkness, thick bolts of lightning stabbing down from those clouds to the ground, and smaller strikes streaking up into the endless grey.

I would have stayed with that view for hours, but I saw something. Below me, perhaps three days' walk in the line of tracks I had been following, towards that volcano, next to the ocean that surrounded it, I saw a glint of light. A patterned flashing of light. Morse code

...---...

S.O.S.

❧

I've said a bit about the flora and the landscape, but not the fauna. That is where the real danger of the hollow earth lies. Mosquitoes the size of my hand, raptors high in the sky with leathery wings, the calls of strange birds and other beasts from the jungle-like forests and… Well, I guess this is no surprise, but the hollow earth is infested with rats and cockroaches. Both large. Both unusually aggressive. There are other animals out there. I can hear them. I see glimpses of them while they shadow me under the cover of the trees for a distance. They must be unused to man and do not know what to make of me. But the cockroaches, twelve inches long and weighing three pounds, and rats the size of small dogs are not so shy.

As I stood there reveling in the magnificence of the view, something scuttled out of a hole hidden between two boulders and made a beeline for me. At first, I had no idea what it was, but had the Colt 45 in hand just in case. When I got a look at its shiny black carapace and its antennae, it became clear that it was a freakishly large cockroach, it's mandible snapping together and its antennae whipping around as it came for me. I holstered the Colt and switched to the machete and was glad that it was easily dispatched. But then the hole erupted, a nightmare of cockroaches pouring out. I backed up knowing that I could dispatch a dozen or two of the beasts, but hundreds? Thousands? The collective sound of their snapping mandibles and clicking legs became a nightmarish hiss. The group stopped momentarily to consume the one I dispatched, the noise of it turning my stomach, before continuing towards me.

I ran.

❧

"*You will encounter weather like you have never imagined. The Earth's atmosphere is only twelve kilometers thick. In the inside, it reaches five thousand kilometers all the way to the central sun making for thunderstorms of a size and a fury to humble anything an outsider has seen.*"

The monster cockroaches were fast, faster than I, and slowly gained as I ran down the hill in the direction of the S.O.S. beacon. I soon lost sight of it as I entered another valley, the snapping of mandibles driving me on, my breath coming in ragged gasps, my lungs burning.

I considered running for the trees, but cockroaches have no trouble climbing. I heard a sharp snap of a mandible, much too close for comfort, and felt it scrape my boot heel. I ran faster and crested another hill, finding the storm that I had spotted earlier was closer than I thought.

I could feel the rumbling thunder in my chest, the rain ahead of me pouring down in sheets, the flashes of lightning nearly blinding me, the smell of ozone filling my nose. I veered to my right and headed towards it, slowing down a little to sheathe the machete and get a good grip on the metal cane.

The delay cost me a bite to my calf, and I redoubled my efforts.

Eiffel demonstrated how to use the cane, slowly and carefully in the hollow earth hall while we sipped wine and ate cheese. Doing it at a full run was something quite different.

A twist of the pole at the end and a pull and it telescoped to twice its length with a sharp point at the end. The wind hit me, slowing me down, more mandibles scraping at my heels, cutting through my pants. The land was starting to shake with the thunder, my head a constant ringing of it. Another twist at the top and a pull and it telescoped further until it was a solid six feet tall. It was awkward to carry as I headed right into the storm, the cold sheets of rain a blessing in my overheated conditions.

The next part was all timing. As I ran, I held what is now a metal pole high as the ozone in the air began to burn at my nostrils. The lightning came quick and close, a strike twenty yards away and then one ten yards away. My vision was marred by afterimages of the lightning, and I could barely hear a thing but the ringing in my ears and the snap, snap of the cockroach mandibles. My hat had fallen, held on by the stampede strap, and I felt a strange sensation on the top of my head, a sharp tingling, and the smell of ozone was overwhelming. I stabbed the metal pole into the ground and kept running. The lightning crashed down, connecting with the metal pole when I was but ten feet in front of it. I went flying and fell in a jumble on the tall, wet grass.

I struggled to get up, pulled the machete, looking around, ready to fight. The scent of burned cockroach overwhelmed the scent of ozone, and I saw the lightning had taken care of my pursuers, a mess of antennae, carapaces, and legs strewn about. I saw the survivors scuttling away back out of the storm. I hunkered down, hiding under my hat as the rain pelted me, the metal pole taking a few more strikes, until the storm finally passed.

~

The rats don't hunt in packs, thankfully. They came at me one at a time, sneaking through the grass or lying in wait in my path. They weighed twenty to thirty pounds, and after the storm passed and I continued my trek to the S.O.S, I was attacked and dispatched several every hour. They are brutish, muscular things with fangs the length of my thumb. I won't bore you with the details of the endless encounters; suffice it to say that I have taken to walking with both the Colt and the machete in hand and both have gotten good use and my ammo is fairly depleted.

The land unfolded, each reveal as spectacular as the last. At one point I turned back, looking the way I had come, and saw a mighty volcano, twice the height of Everest, behind me, past my entry point, just visible through the grey sky. This track of un-forested valleys I had been following was the result of that volcano, its flow seared the ground some hundreds of years ago and the forest had not filled it back in.

Which was just as well, I knew the forest held more dangers than oversized rats and cockroaches.

~

I spent what felt like three days traveling to that flashing light. I would trek until exhaustion overcame me, following Verne's tracks at times, then losing them and finding them again. Inevitably when it was time to stop, I would find a camp made in the lightning blasted areas complete with a fire pit and a stack of wood. I would bless his foresight, start a large fire to keep the cockroaches and rats away, and sleep a few hours.

When I finally arrived at the S.O.S beacon, I was quite a bit worse for the wear. Exhausted with numerous scrapes, cuts, and bites, feeling every bit of my forty-one years.

I wanted nothing more than to lie down for a week, prefer-ably in a nice hotel with room service—Paris would do nicely. But what I found was not the end of my journey. The once distant volcano was now close, and I could smell sulphur. A large body of dark water stood between me and the volcano. It was on the shore of this large lake where I found the source of the S.O.S. It was not a man, but a strange device.

It was a wooden box, the size of my hand, the top removed and a small mirror protruding. Inside were a series of gears and springs, like a larger version of what is inside of a watch, and on the side was a handle, like on a phonograph but smaller, to crank the thing. It clicked and turned, making the mirror move up and down in the Morse code pattern for S.O.S.

The shore of the lake was made up of black cinders and rocks, the evidence of volcanic activity having not been taken over by the unrelentingly verdant nature of the hollow earth. The land was irregular, the black rock looking like huge pieces of overbaked chocolate cake, forming folds in the land. I sheathed the machete and explored, the Colt in hand. I had to be careful, the rocks were sharp, the land being brand new, geologically speaking.

It didn't take long to find Jules Verne. He had made camp in a small cave formed by the undulating land. He had a Colt revolver pointed at me as I rounded the corner. "Who are you?" he asked as he pulled the hammer back.

～

*J*ules Verne stank. There is no other word to describe it. Yes, he smelled like a man that had not bathed in far too long—as did I—but his scent was much worse than that. I smelled the iron of blood, urine, and something much fouler.

"My name is Marco Walker, Monsieur Verne," I said. "I was sent by Gustav Eiffel to rescue you."

He relaxed and breathed out a sigh, but his eyes kept darting around. "Of course, of course. Who else could be down here?" He then chuckled in a way that made my skin crawl. "I am afraid things have not gone well. I can't walk." He pointed to his thigh which was heavily bandaged. "And some creature has taken what I came for." He pointed towards the water. "I am afraid the task before you is too much to ask of any man."

I smiled as best I could, for I was exhausted and battered, and was hoping to find Verne with the prize he had come for and be facing nothing more than a trek back to the tunnel fending off rabid, forty-pound rats and swarms of hand-sized cockroaches. "Perhaps you should explain it to me then."

~

*T*he only good news Verne had was that there was a way to keep the cockroaches away. It involved slathering yourself with a fetid substance that was a combination of rotting cockroach innards and a musky flower he had found at the edge of the forest. So, I promptly followed his prescription, for the rocks were favored by the bugs, and soon I was as rank as he.

Next up was the creature that had stolen the Scepter of Khufu. He told me briefly of how he obtained it, enshrined in a small pyramid the Egyptians had built down here many miles distant. The tale he told and the dangers he faced alone raised my estimation of him by no small degree. Not to mention that he did this at the age of sixty-one, twenty years my senior. He had stopped here to rest, having barely escaped his last rat attack and knowing that the rats did not like the sharp lava flows. A thing that he described as "half fish, half animal" had crawled out of the water and taken the scepter before he knew what was happening.

"And have you seen this creature since?" I asked, my nose overwhelmed from the stench of the two of us. It was quite painful to inhale through my nose, so insulting to the senses was the odor.

"Only glimpses," he said, pointing out towards a small island of black volcanic land about two hundred yards in the water. At that moment, the volcano set out a gout of lava high into the sky, I could feel the earth vibrate under my feet, and watched as the hot lava splashed into the water, founts of steam rising. "It is amphibious, and I believe that is where it is keeping the scepter."

"Any other signs of life in this water?" I asked.

Verne nodded solemnly, his hand rubbing at his grey beard. "There are fish, and at times I see thrashing in the water as if great beasts are fighting just below the surface."

I nodded and walked away from Verne towards the forest.

"What are you going to do?" he yelled after me.

"Build a raft."

~

The central sun is maddening. There is no night, there is no day really, either. On the outside, the sun's position is ever changing, the day flowing from dawn to sunset. On the inside it never moves, always right above you, always telling your body that it is noon.

Building the raft was hard work. Trekking to the forest, some miles distant, chopping off branches the size of my arm with the machete, which was not designed for the task, and then hauling them back to the lake—I have decided to call it a lake even though it was the size of a small ocean. The lack of salt in the water did it for me. It is such things that occupied my addled mind.

After many trips, Verne made me stop, told me it was "night" and that we should rest. I laughed at him and headed back out. At the forest, I moved farther in, struggling to find branches that were even remotely straight that I could also reach. I also liked the cool of the forest and how it shielded from the sun above. I wandered farther in, not really thinking about it.

Now, I had heard sounds coming from these forests. Great roars, sharp cries, and the calling of birds. I knew things lived here, and judging from the creatures I had run into thus far, I knew they must be mighty things.

I was beginning to think better of my walk among the trees and the ferns when I saw it. A footprint, a bare human footprint. For a moment, I thought it must be my own footprint, but I wore boots and this foot was much larger than mine. I stopped, the forest quiet, wondering who else could be here, how they had gotten here, and what they might think of me.

I heard a rustling and sank low, backing up against one of the mighty trees. And then I saw it. A man. A beast. I could not tell. It was some twenty yards distant through the trees. It was shaped like a man but had hair all over its body, its hands large and crude, its head small.

I did not move. I did not breathe, and then it stopped and sniffed the air, turning towards me.

Our eyes met and it froze. Those eyes were so human and yet... They were not like any eyes I had ever seen. Wild and wise at the same time.

I blinked, and then he was gone. I made my way out of the forest as quickly and quietly as possible. I jogged back to Verne, who had almost completed assembling the raft, and told him what I had seen.

He put his hand to my forehead and said, "You are fevered, that is all. There are no men down here." He convinced me pretty well of it, but then again, I wanted to be convinced. We rested for a few hours, my dreams full of overgrown forests and man-beasts.

~

The island was maybe ten feet in diameter, a rocky protrusion of lava poking its head up above the water. The lake was shallow here and I polled my way slowly towards it, keeping a careful lookout for those creatures he had seen thrashing in the water. I looked back at Jules Verne, he leaned on the crutches I had created for him and gave me an encouraging wave. The thing I had seen—or not seen—in the forest, the man-beast, had spooked me. This underworld had things more mysterious and challenging than oversized cockroaches and rats.

I stepped off the raft and onto the land, my foot crunching on the black cinders. I pulled the raft up and started looking around. I found fish skeletons strewn about; these too were large. I estimated the smallest of these fish to be three feet long, and the skeletons revealed that they had sharp teeth. I looked back to the raft, glad to have stayed out of these waters.

I circumnavigated the small piece of land, finding nothing more than the fish skeletons, and then took a step inland. From behind me I heard a hiss and turned to see Verne's thief crawling out of the water. It was a strange thing, not quite fish, not quite mammal. My stomach tightened and my hand went to the Colt holstered on my hip.

The creature was about four feet long from head to tail, with the scales, fins, and the tail of a fish, but it also had four small legs with webbed hands. Its mouth was shaped more like an animal's with sharp teeth and a tongue. It was a mottled blue and grey.

My breath caught when I saw its eyes. These were not the flat, lifeless eyes of a fish, but animal eyes with blue irises and intelligence shining through.

"Easy, friend," I said, holding my hands up. "You took something from us, I'm just going to get it back."

I took a step backwards, towards the center of the island, and the amphibian opened its mouth wide, showing me its teeth, and hissed again, its breath fetid and fishy.

This was his lake, his home, I was the invader. I understood its position. As I didn't know what it was, it didn't know what I was either, otherwise it would have attacked already.

I twisted around and glanced behind me and saw a collection of objects. Some small, some large, all of them shiny. A few silver coins, a small mirror, bits of metal—all debris of man's visits to the hollow earth. I caught a glimpse of gold in the midst. The amphibian was like a magpie and couldn't help but collect these shiny things.

"How about a trade, friend?"

I carefully pulled the small wooden S.O.S box out of my backpack, removed the lid, the mirror popping up, and I slowly cranked it. As I did this, first the creature backed into the dark water, but then when the mirror popped up, its blue eyes widened and I swear there was a smile on its face.

When the mirror started moving, the tick-tick of the clock-work mechanism moving it up and down, the creature was enraptured.

I slowly moved back, grabbed the gold scepter and moved back to the raft.

~

I must finish this quickly, Verne is anxious to get back to the surface; he needs a real doctor to look at that leg. Our journey back to the tunnel was free of cockroaches, thanks to his stinking salve, and full of rat attacks.

The going was slow, Verne could not move fast on his crutches, and the days—such as they were under that unmoving sun—we couldn't make it to one of his fire rings, we built another. But we had a shadow for the trip back; something, someone pacing us from the edge of the forest. The man-beast I had seen, perhaps.

The sun is still maddening, with its eternal position directly overhead, but I am starting to like this land. I have decided to not go back.

"But, Marco," Verne said when I told him, "the full Hollow Earth Council will be there. Mark Twain, Teddy Roosevelt, Annie Oakley, Gertrude Bell, and all the rest. They will surely want to thank you themselves, welcome you into our beloved society."

I could imagine them all in the cavernous room with the best wine and cheeses France has to offer, companionship of great men and women, a celebration beyond measure. I shook my head, my eye straying to the mechanized moles that had brought us down here. My stomach turned and my knees got weak at the thought of two more days locked in it.

"You go, I quite like it here. I will get the base camp started and I'll see you in a few months."

He prepares himself for the journey as I write this. The telling of the tale is a requirement for membership into the Hollow Earth Society, and while I do not want to return to the surface, I quite fancy the idea of being a full member. This land is worth protecting.

Besides, my body aches from this adventure but my heart soars. I feel like a young man when I explored the wilds of Alaska, having no idea what was around the bend or over the next ridge. I feel more alive than I have in a decade. This hollow earth is for me.

Soon he will be gone, locked in the belly of that smoke-spewing coffin, and I will have this grand land to myself. Eiffel was right, he promised me an adventure beyond my imagination, and I know that it has just begun.

MORE ADVENTURE?

There are more Marco Walker Hollow Earth adventures coming soon. If you want to know when the next one comes out, your best bet is to sign up for my newsletter at RobertJMcCarter.com/newsletter. You'll get some free ebooks and you'll find out when the story is available. Or go to RobertJMcCarter.com/HollowEarth for a complete list of Hollow Earth stories.

If you want more adventure, I've got a two other series you might want to check out:

WOODY AND JUNE VERSUS THE APOCALYPSE

Love and the Apocalypse

When Woody Beckman meets June Medina, neither expects the adventures that will follow. Dedicated go-it-alone survivors, they've learned not to trust anyone in post-zombie-apocalypse Arizona.

But when regular-guy Woody must save tough-as-nails June, they realize that to survive they must learn to trust each other.

As the pair deals with everything from zombies to psychotic, petty, wannabe warlords to the harsh Arizona deserts, they start to realize that they might just prefer facing this crazy world together.

A story of adventure and love and taking things (even the apocalypse) in stride.

There are seven episodes out now with five more coming in 2021. Get the first two episodes for free by joining the fan club or go grab Volume 1 with the first seven episodes!

NEUTRINOMAN & LIGHTNINGIRL: A LOVE STORY

Superheroes... falling in love... saving the world.

Follow Nik Nichols (aka Neutrinoman) and Licia Lopez (aka Lightningirl) on this wild adventure past "happily ever after" into the heart of love while they try to protect the Earth from aliens bent on our destruction. There are two seasons and six episodes out!

Join my newsletter and get the *Meteor Attack!* ebook for free! Find out the latest at Neutrinoman.com

ABOUT THE AUTHOR

Robert J. McCarter is the author of over a dozen novels, nine novellas, and dozens of short stories. He is a finalist for the *Writers of the Future* contest and his stories have appeared or are forthcoming in *The Saturday Evening Post, Pulphouse Fiction Magazine, Fiction River, Andromeda Spaceways Inflight Magazine,* and numerous anthologies.

A recent effort is a serialized novel called *Woody and June Versus the Apocalypse*, a story of adventure and love and taking things (even the apocalypse) in stride. Of his novel, *Seeing Forever*, Kirkus Reviews says, "Sci-fi as it should be: engaging, moving, and grand in scope."

He lives in the mountains of Arizona with his amazing wife and his ridiculously adorable dogs.

Find out more at:
RobertJMcCarter.com

BOOKS BY ROBERT J. MCCARTER

WOODY AND JUNE VERSUS THE APOCALYPSE

- Woody and June versus the Wannabe Warlord
- Woody and June versus the Fungus-Head Zombies
- Woody and June versus the Grand Canyon
- Woody and June versus the Ex
- Woody and June versus the Third Wheel
- Woody and June versus Phantom Company
- Woody and June versus the Daring Rescue
- Volume 1: Episodes 1-7 (all seven episodes for a great price)
- Five more episodes coming in 2021!

Join the Woody and June Fan Club at WoodyAndJune.com

NEUTRINOMAN & LIGHTNINGIRL: A LOVE STORY

- Meteor Attack!
- Toxic Asset
- Protocol X
- Season 1 (Omnibus edition of Episodes 1 - 3)
- Off Book
- Hard Times
- Elemental Factors
- Season 2 (Omnibus edition of Episodes 4-6)

Find out the latest at Neutrinoman.com

SHORT STORES COLLECTIONS

- Life After: Stories of Life, Death, and the Places in Between
- Anomalous Readings: Thirteen Curious and Confounding Tales
- Creatures Featured: Thirteen Stories of Monsters and other Creatures

NOVELS IN THE "GHOST'S MEMOIR" WORLD:

Find out more at ShuffledOff.com

OTHER NOVELS:

- Seeing Forever
- Where the Past Belongs: An Angelica and Ash Time Travel Adventure

For a more information, go to RobertJMcCarter.com